CONTENTS

Stories retold by Maureen Spurgeon

First published 1995 by Brown Watson
The Old Mill, 76 Fleckney Road,
Kibworth Beauchamp,
Leicestershire, England

Reprinted 1996, 1997, 1999, 2000, 2001, 2003, 2005, 2007, 2009

ISBN:978-0-7097-1025-7
©1995 Brown Watson, England

Printed in China

FAIRY TALE
TREASURY

BOOK ONE

Brown Watson
ENGLAND

Hansel and Gretel

In a wooden cabin at the edge of a thick, dark forest, there lived a poor woodcutter and his wife. They had two children — a boy named Hansel, and a girl whose name was Gretel.

Times were very hard, and more often than not, there was barely enough to eat.

"We cannot go on like this, wife!" said the woodcutter, one night.

"And what about the children?" she sobbed. "Suppose we die before they do? Who will look after them?"

"If we leave them in the forest," said the woodcutter, "at least they will have nuts and berries to eat. And noblemen out hunting might find them and give them a home."

Next morning, there was only a crust of bread for the two children to share before they all set out for the forest. Only Gretel saw Hansel putting it into his pocket . . .

Then Hansel crumbled the bread, ready to drop a piece every few paces as they went through the forest. Now, he thought, they could find their way back home!

After they had gone quite a distance, the woodcutter made a fire to keep the children warm. Stiff and tired, they lay down, hardly caring where they were.

Next thing they knew, it was completely dark!

"We're lost!" Gretel kept crying. "How can we see the pieces of bread to guide us home now, Hansel?"

On and on they walked through the forest, their feet becoming blistered and sore. Suddenly, Hansel stopped. "Look, Gretel! Smoke coming from a chimney!"

Gretel could see nothing. But as they came nearer, the children saw a funny-looking cottage with a pretty little garden, and flowers that sparkled like sugar candy!

"Mmm, delicious!" cried Gretel, picking a leaf. "Try some, Hansel!" But he was already taking bites of sponge cake tiles and wondering if the marzipan roof tasted as good!

Suddenly, they heard a voice,
cracked and wheezing.
"Who is there? A little mouse?
Who is nibbling at my house?"

It was the ugliest old woman they had ever seen! Gretel turned to run, but the woman spoke kindly.

"Hungry, are we? Come inside, I've plenty of food to spare!"

Hansel and Gretel had never seen such a meal! How could they have guessed that the kind old woman was really a witch who lay in wait for children?

"A pity they are so thin," she cackled to herself as they slept. "Still, that makes the boy light enough for me to lock him up in my cellar without any trouble!"

Early next morning, Gretel was awoken by a hard kick.

"Get busy, you little wretch!" screamed the witch. "Fetch some water and light the fire!"

Gretel was too frightened to disobey.

"You can cook a meal for your brother," the witch went on. "I want him fattened up before I eat him!"

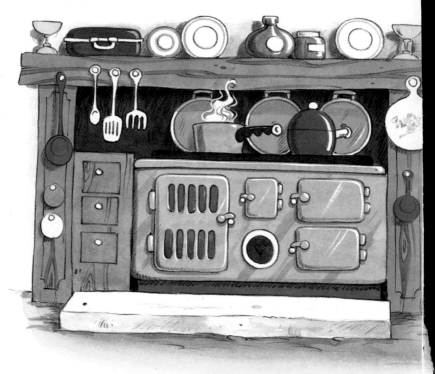

And every day, the witch came to see how fat Hansel was getting.

"Let's feel your arm," she would scream. Hansel always held up one of the bones Gretel passed to him.

Lucky for Hansel, the witch could not see further than the end of her nose.

"Too thin!" she would screech. "Still too thin!"

At last, the witch decided she could wait no longer.

"Girl!" she screamed. "Stoke the fire and get the oven hot! Fat or thin, I mean to eat your brother!"

Hansel was amazed to see Gretel obeying so calmly.

"Please," she said after a while, "will you check to see if the oven is hot enough?"

The witch dashed forward at once, rubbing her hands greedily. And the moment she put her head inside, Gretel pushed as hard as she could — and slammed the door shut!

With trembling fingers, Gretel
unbolted the entrance to the
cellar.

"Come out, Hansel!" she cried.
"The witch cannot harm us, now!"

But Hansel refused to leave the cottage without taking as much of the witch's treasure as they could. They would never need to worry about being cold or hungry again.

How happy they were to hear
their mother and father calling
them through the forest. They had
been searching for the children
from the day they had left them.

Laughing and crying, it was hard to believe they were all together.

"At last," said the woodcutter, "we can go home without any fears. We are a family again."

Aladdin

Once upon a time, in one of the very oldest cities in ancient China, there lived a poor widow, and her son, who was called Aladdin.

Aladdin was a good boy, always bright and cheerful and ready to help people whenever he could.

And to help his mother, he would go to the market once or twice a week.

One day in the market place, a man said he had a job for Aladdin. "You will be well paid," he said.

The man led Aladdin to a secret cave. "I want you to climb down this rope," he said. "I am too fat to get through the hole myself, you see."

When his feet touched the floor of the cave, he could hardly believe what he saw! Chests and boxes, all filled with treasure!

"Stop dreaming!" shouted the man, his voice hard and cruel. "Start tying everything to the rope, so that I can pull it up here!"

It was hard work, tying on all the treasures. But Aladdin kept thinking of the money he had been promised, and all he could buy for his mother!

My turn, now!" cried Aladdin,
when he had finished.

The man tugged the rope
away.

"Set you free to let everyone
know my secret?"

And with an evil laugh, the man thundered away, leaving Aladdin trapped in the underground cave with no food, no water, no money . . . nothing, except one thing . . .

The lamp did not look very special. But Aladdin began rubbing it. At once, there was a whooshing sound, and a bright flash of light!

"I am the genie of the lamp!" said a deep voice, the huge eyes of the genie twinkling at the look of amazement on Aladdin's face. "Your wish is my command!"

"I'd like something to take to my mother!" Aladdin burst out. Next minute, he was in another treasure cave, even bigger than the first!

"Take whatever you wish," smiled the genie. "Then my magic carpet will take you home. Just rub the lamp whenever you need me, and I will come at once."

Aladdin's mother could hardly believe what she saw!

"No more worries about having enough money for food!" he told her proudly. "We're rich, now!"

Before long, Aladdin and his mother had the most wonderful mansion which the genie built by magic! Even the Emperor was impressed by what he saw!

Such a handsome, wealthy young man would be the ideal husband for his daughter, he thought. And how proud Aladdin's mother was to see her son marry a beautiful princess!

By this time, the man who had left Aladdin in the underground cave was so jealous! How, he wondered, had Aladdin got his riches? He decided to watch him, every hour of the day.

At last, his patience was rewarded. As soon as he saw Aladdin rubbing his magic lamp and the genie appearing, he guessed what the secret was! The magic lamp should be his, he decided!

He put on the clothes of a pedlar, and went to the street where Aladdin lived.

"New lamps for old!" he cried, ringing a bell. "New lamps for old!"

It sounded a bargain to the emperor's daughter. But Aladdin was very angry, and guessed who had taken the lamp.

Sure enough, at the market next day — the man was there, selling the treasures the genie had got for him. Aladdin knew he would not risk bringing the magic lamp to the market . . .

So, he followed him home, waiting for his chance to snatch the magic lamp, give it a rub and make the genie appear!

"Take this man away to a far-off land!" he commanded.

"Very good, Master!" roared the genie. "Your wish is my command!"

The man tried to escape, but the magic power of the genie was stronger than any man!

How he wished then that he had not been so greedy!

As for Aladdin, he overjoyed to see the genie ag welcoming him home like the t friend he was!

From now on, he said, the g should live like a real person.

"Such kindness is all that was needed to free me!" cried the genie. But he still worked his magic for Aladdin to help the poor, as he and his mother had once been.

The Three Little Pigs

THERE was once a family of three little pigs.

They were very happy little pigs — except for one thing.

Each of them did so wish that he could have a proper home of his own.

It was all they had ever hoped for, all they had ever dreamed about.

Then, one day, the first little pig said: "We have talked about having a home of our own long enough. Why not set to work, with each of us building a house for ourselves?"

"Good idea!" said the second little pig.

"I shall start at once!" cried the third little pig. And off he went, as fast as his trotters could carry him.

Before long, he came across a
man raking through a whole pile
of straw.

"Good man," said the little pig,
"may I have some straw to build
myself a house?"

The man laughed. "Yes, if you are sure that is what you want," he said. "Take as much as you like."
The little pig was so pleased.

All day long, the little pig worked so hard, until, at last, the little house of straw really looked cosy enough to live in for always.

But, as the sun set, and the little pig sat thinking what a nice little home he had, there came three loud knocks at the door. Then, a fearsome shadow appeared.....

"Little pig!" growled the wolf.
"Little pig! Let me come in!"

"No, no!" squealed the pig. "By
the hair on my chinny-chin-chin, I
will NOT let you in!"

"Then," roared the wolf, "I'll HUFF and I'll PUFF and I'll BLOW your house in!"

So, he HUFFED . . . . .

And, he PUFFED . . . . .

And he BLEW the house in!
That poor little pig!
He only just managed to run
away in time.

Whilst all this was going on, the second little pig had been busy, too. He had decided that he would like his house built of wood.

"Good man," he said to a woodcutter, "may I have some wood to build myself a house?"

"Wood, to build a house?" laughed the woodcutter. "Take as much as you like!"

The second little pig worked
hard all day long, sawing and
banging and hammering — until,
at last, the house of wood was
almost ready to live in.

But no sooner had he settled in, than there was a knock at the door.

"Little pig!" roared the wolf. "Little pig! Let me come in!"

"No, no!" cried the pig. "By the hair on my chinny chin-chin, I will not let you in!"

"Then," roared the wolf, "I'll HUFF, and I'll PUFF, and I'll BLOW your house in!"

So, he HUFFED . . . . **And,** PUFFED . . . .

And, he BLEW that house **in !**
That poor little pig! He **only i**
managed to run away in **time !**

And as for the first little pig — he had been just as busy as the other two. But first, he had spent time looking at other houses. They all seemed to be made of bricks . . . . .

So, off he went to find a builder.

"Good man," he said, "will you let me have some bricks to build a house?"

"I think so," answered the man. "You will also need some sand and cement."

Well, the first little pig worked so hard! And by the end of the day, even the builder said he had built a fine house to live in.

That evening, there was a loud banging at the door.

"Let us in!" squealed a voice.

"The wolf has blown our lovely new houses in!"

They were hardly inside the little brick house when there was a loud knock at the door.

"Little pig! Let me come in!" And this time, nobody answered.

The wolf was so angry!

"I'll HUFF," he roared, "and I'll PUFF, and I'll BLOW your house in!"

So, he HUFFED.

And, he PUFFED.

But he could NOT blow the house in! So, he climbed up on the roof! He thought he could get into the house by going down through the chimney!

But the little pigs soon had a fire burning. So, by the time he had finished, the wolf was sorry he had ever tried getting into the strong little house built of bricks!

With a loud cry, the wolf ran off, never to be seen again!

After that nobody was happier than the three little pigs, living in a strong safe house of bricks, all of their own.

Stories I have read

Goldilocks and the Three Bears

Red Riding Hood

Snow White and the Seven Dwarfs

The Ugly Duckling

The Wizard of Oz

Pinocchio